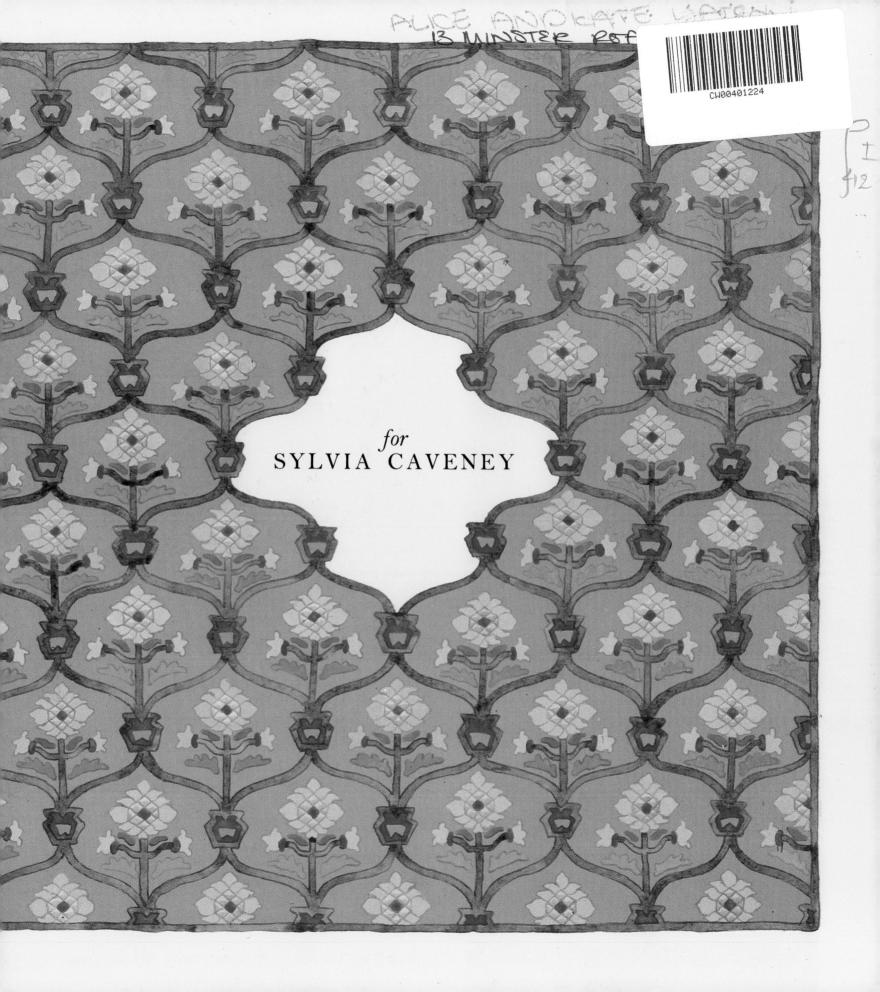

for
SYLVIA CAVENEY

VASILY &
THE DRAGON
AN EPIC RUSSIAN FAIRY TALE
TOLD & ILLUSTRATED BY
SIMON STERN

First published in Great Britain by
Pelham Books Ltd
44 Bedford Square
London WC1B 3DU
1982

ISBN 0 7207 1331 5

Filmset by BAS Printers Limited, Over Wallop, Hampshire
Printed and bound by New Interlitho, Milan, Italy

PELHAM BOOKS

IN A CERTAIN KINGDOM, IN

a certain land, lived Marko the Rich, who had more money than he could count.

One night as Marko lay sleeping, he heard a voice; and this is what it said:

Marko the Rich prepare yourself,
Marko the Rich bestir yourself!
Tomorrow night two guests will come:
Holy St Nicholas will be one.
The other who knocks upon your door
Will be Lord God, the King of all!

When Marko woke up the next morning he called his wife.

'Wife, wife, order the cooks to prepare a feast, for tonight God and St Nicholas will be our guests!'

Then he summoned his steward.

'Steward, have red cloth spread for twenty miles around my house. Let every yard of ground be covered, not a blade of grass be seen, for tonight the Lord God himself will be our guest.'

So carpets and cloth were spread about, the feast was prepared, and the whole house waited for the guests to arrive.

That very night two old beggars came to the house. Barefoot and cold, their clothes in rags, they dragged themselves across the red carpets to the door behind which Marko the Rich sat waiting for the Lord God.

'Peace be with you, Marko the Rich! Give us a bite to eat, grant us a bed for the night, and heaven will reward you.'

'What, you vermin!' cried Marko. 'Who sent you here with your rags and crutches? Here I sit, waiting for the Lord God to visit me, and you bring your filth into my house! Be off, or I'll set the dogs on you.'

Now Marko had an only child, a girl of four named Anastasya. She took pity on the two old men and begged her father to let them sleep in the cowshed.

'Very well,' said Marko. 'But mind they don't show their faces until morning.' And he sat on, waiting for his guests. But no one came; and at last, as midnight struck, Marko stamped upstairs to bed, vowing never again to believe in dreams.

When all the household were asleep, Anastasya crept out to the cowshed and peeped in. There were the two beggars lying in the straw. Suddenly she heard a whirring and a scratching, and a voice spoke from the far corner.

'Has the Lord God laid down to rest here?'

'Yes, what do you want?'

'Lord, in the village a boy is born to a poor woman. By what name shall he be called, and what will be his fortune?'

Then the older beggar spoke.

'Vasily the Unlucky shall be his name
And great indeed shall be his fame;
For this is the fortune I presage:
Before he's sixteen years of age
He will possess all Marko's wealth,
Though Marko the Rich still lives himself.'

Anastasya stayed to hear no more. She ran to her father's bed-chamber.

'Father, come at once! God and Saint Nicholas are in the cowshed!' When she told him all she had heard, Marko ran down and flung open the cowshed door; but the beggars had gone.

'Harness my three black mares,' cried Marko; and he jumped into the coachman's seat and galloped off towards the village. There in a hut a poor woman had given birth to a baby boy.

'Woman,' said Marko, 'sell me your child.'

'Why sir, he is not for sale.'

So Marko began to persuade her and spoke kindly.

'My good woman, think of your little ones, whom you can scarcely feed as it is. I am rich and I have no son. I will bring him up as my own, and pay you a thousand roubles as well.'

So in the end the parents agreed and Marko wrapped the child in fox furs and drove away.

But instead of taking the child back to his house, Marko drove up into the mountains until he came to a deep ravine. There he stopped. He carried the child to the very edge, seized it by its legs and hurled it into the depths, saying: 'Now let him take my wealth if he can.'

The next day two merchants came along the same road to pay Marko the Rich some money they owed him.

Snow had fallen in the night and lay thick on the ground. As they passed the ravine they heard a child crying. They ran to the edge and peered down. Below them was a ledge on which green grass grew and flowers bloomed, though the snow was knee-deep all around. On the ledge sat a child, playing with the flowers and whimpering.

'This is a miracle,' they said; 'he must be a holy child.'

They clambered down to the ledge, wrapped the child in a fur coat, returned to the carriage and went on their way.

As they drove, the two friends talked. 'We must not let Marko see him. He has no son of his own, and if he sees the child he'll want to keep it,' said one. So it was agreed.

When they arrived at Marko's house, Marko lit the samovar and they all drank tea; but the merchants were afraid that the child might freeze in the carriage, so first one, then the other went outside to make sure that all was well.

'What have you got in that carriage of yours that's so precious?' asked Marko.

They did not want to tell him, but in the end he wheedled it out of them.

'My good friends,' he said, 'give the child to me! I have no sons and I need the boy. Besides, you still owe me money and if I wished I could make you repay the whole amount. But if you give the child to me I will cancel your debts and sell you new goods.'

Well, in the end the merchants gave in. Marko took the child in his arms, then gave him to his wife to look after.

But Marko only wished the child dead. After three days had passed, he took the boy from the cradle while his wife slept. Then he put the baby in a casket, so that no one should see what he was carrying, and drove off in his carriage until he came to a deep river.

'The ravine did not kill you, but the river will,' he said; and he flung the casket in and left the boy to drown.

But the casket did not sink.

It floated down the river and out into the sea. Storms raged,

winds blew, but still the casket floated on. At last it passed by an island on which there was a monastery.

A monk, who happened to be out fishing, saw the casket bobbing about in the water. He took a boat hook and fished it up. Imagine his surprise when he found a baby lying inside.

He took the child at once to the abbot.

'He is God's gift to us!' the abbot exclaimed, and then and there he arranged for the child to be baptised. The monks became his godfathers and the abbot gave him the name of Vasily the Unlucky, because he had been thrown into the sea to drown.

So the years went by and Vasily grew up in the care of the monks. When he was fifteen the old abbot sent for him.

'My son,' he said, 'for fifteen years you have lived with us, although you are not a monk and do not wear the brown habit. Now the time has come for you to go out into the wide world.'

It happened at that time that Marko the Rich was travelling across the seas on business and stopped at the island. While the monks made him welcome Marko noticed that one of them was not dressed like the others.

'Who is that young man?' he asked.

'His name is Vasily the Unlucky,' answered the abbot. 'Fifteen years ago we found him floating in a casket in the sea. We brought him up as our son, but now it is time for him to go into the wide world.'

'Let me see the casket,' said Marko the Rich.

When he saw it, he recognized it at once and knew for certain that the young man was his own adopted son whom he had tried

to drown all those years ago.

'Abbot,' he said, 'I need a young man like that. Give the boy to me and I will make him chief clerk and put him in charge of all my treasure.'

'Gladly,' said the abbot. 'It will be a good chance for the boy,' he thought.

Then Marko sat down and wrote a letter. This is what it said:

'Wife: when you receive this letter, take the youth who brings it to our soap works. When you pass near the boiling cauldron, push him in. Do not fail in this, or I will punish you severely.'

Then he sealed the letter and gave it to Vasily:

'Take one of my ships, go to my house and deliver this letter to my wife. She will know what to do.'

So Marko continued his voyage and Vasily the Unlucky took ship for Marko's country and set out for Marko's house.

But it was not long before he lost his way; as night began to fall, he came to a dark forest. He walked and walked. In the distance he saw a light flickering and going towards it he found two old beggars warming

their hands before the fire.

'Greetings Vasily the Unlucky! What brings you to this dark forest?'

'I am taking a letter to the wife of Marko the Rich, but I have lost my way,' the boy replied.

'Show us the letter.'

The elder of the two beggars took the letter, blew on it, and gave it back.

'Follow this path,' he said, 'until you come to the crossroads. The road to the left goes over the mountains, where there is a deep ravine. Take that road and you will come to the house of Marko the Rich.'

Vasily did as the old beggar directed. He took the road over the mountains, and came to the house of Marko the Rich. There at the door sat Anastasya, embroidering on her silver frame.

'What brings you and who sent you?' she asked.

'Marko the Rich sent me. I bring a letter for his wife.'

When Marko's wife opened the letter, this is what it said:

'*Wife: when you receive this letter, marry the youth who brings it to our daughter. Do not fail in this, or I will punish you severely.*'

What could she do? She had no choice in the matter. A feast was prepared, Vasily the Unlucky was dressed up in fine clothes and they were married the next day.

At last Marko the Rich returned home.

'Well, wife, did you do as my letter said?'

'Yes, husband, I married the youth to our daughter Anastasya as you commanded.'

Marko the Rich was so vexed that his teeth itched. He spat in his wife's face and shouted, 'What have you done, you stupid woman?'

She pulled out the letter and showed it to him. When he saw that the letter had been changed, he thought:

'Nothing I do can harm this boy. Some lucky charm protects him. But I will send him to a place so terrible that nothing can save him from destruction.'

So he called Vasily to him.

'Vasily the Unlucky,' he said, 'now that you are my son-in-law I require you to do something for me. Beyond the thrice ninth land, beyond the thrice tenth kingdom, is the world's end. There the Heathen Dragon lives. Go and ask him how much money I have, for I myself can no longer count it.'

When Anastasya heard what her father had commanded she wept bitterly and begged him to change his mind, but all to no avail. Early the next morning Vasily said his prayers, took some

biscuits in his knapsack and set out.

He walked and walked, a long way or a short way, until he came to the thrice tenth kingdom. There he found a wide river and a ferryman who took people across for no payment.

'Ferryman, I want to cross the river,' said Vasily.

'I will take you young man; but first tell me where you are going.'

'I am going to the world's end to visit the Heathen Dragon.'

'Ah, dear brother; I have been looking for such a passenger for a long time. Remind the Dragon of me when you see him. For thirty years now I have travelled back and forth across this river for no payment. I have no flesh left on my hands; they are nothing but bone and across the bone the blood runs in streams. Ask the Dragon who will take my place.'

'Certainly I will ask him,' Vasily replied.

So the ferryman took Vasily across and he went on his way.

Presently he came to a pillar built of gold coins, so tall that it reached from the earth to the sky.

'Vasily the Unlucky where are you going?' said a voice.

Vasily looked about to see who was speaking, but there was no one in sight.

'It is I, the pillar of gold, who calls you. Tell me, where are you going?'

'I am going to the world's end to visit the Heathen Dragon.'

'When you see him, remind him of me. Ask him, to whom do I belong?'

'Certainly I will ask him,' Vasily replied.

He went on and on and at last he came to the world's end, where the Heathen Dragon's palace stood. Instead of a door it had a mouth, and smoke came out of the windows.

Just then the Heathen Dragon was not at home. He had flown out into the wide world to eat people alive. But in the farthermost room Vasily found an old woman sitting in a big armchair. She was the Dragon's grandmother.

'Fie, fie! What comes nigh?' she said. 'Who are you, and what brings you to this accursed place?'

'Little grandmother, Marko the Rich sent me to ask the Heathen Dragon how much money he has, for he himself can no longer count it.'

'Alas, my boy, he will eat you up! Unless I ask him for you, he will certainly devour you.'

Vasily the Unlucky fell on his knees before the old woman.

'Little grandmother, help me! Do not let me die a bitter death here.'

'Eh, eh, you're a good lad, and I've a mind to spare you. Very well, I'll ask him myself.'

'Then please ask him this, too. On my way I came to a wide river. The ferryman there has travelled back and forth for thirty years for no payment. Who will take his place?'

'All right. I'll ask him that as well.'

'Little grandmother, ask him one more thing. On my way I saw a pillar of gold, which reached from the earth to the sky. To whom does it belong?'

'Well, well, you're full of questions,' said the old woman. 'Never mind, I'll ask them all. Quick now, under the bed. I hear my grandson coming.'

Hardly had Vasily crawled under the bed than the Heathen Dragon flew in at the window. He had come home hungry, for he had found no one to eat.

'Fie, fie! What comes nigh? I smell Russian flesh!'

So saying he began to sniff about the room, licking his chops and clashing his iron teeth.

'Come, come, little grandson,' said the old woman. 'You've flown all over Russia, and the smell is still in your nostrils. Lie down on the bed, and I'll scratch your head.'

So the Heathen Dragon lay down on the bed, and

the old woman began to scratch him. Presently she said:

'Little grandson, answer me one question. In a certain land lives Marko the Rich. How much money does he possess?'

'Eh, little grandmother, that's a hard one. He has so much that even I cannot count it. There is enough to cover the ground for twenty miles around his house in coins an inch deep. Now let me sleep, for I'm tired.'

'Little grandson, answer me one more question. In a certain land is a wide river. There the ferryman has travelled back and forth for thirty years for no payment. Who will take his place?'

'Eh, little grandmother, that's an easy one. The first man who takes the oar from his hand; that is the man who will take his place. Now be quiet, I want to sleep.'

'Little grandson, answer me one last question. In a certain land there stands a pillar of gold, reaching from the earth to the sky. To whom will it belong?'

'As for that, little grandmother, it already belongs to some-one. Marko the Rich has a son, and that gold is his.'

With that the Heathen Dragon closed his eyes and started to snore, making a noise like twenty saucepans boiling at once.

The old woman let Vasily out from under the bed and he took his leave of her and thanked her for her help.

Presently he came again to the pillar of gold coins.

'Vasily the Unlucky, did you ask my question?'

'Yes indeed I did. You belong to the son of Marko the Rich.'

At once the pillar clinked and clanked and rattled down in a heap at Vasily's feet.

'Now I belong to you,' it said.

'I am not Marko's son, but his son-in-law,' thought Vasily. So he did not take the treasure with him, but let it lie there.

When he came to the wide river, the ferryman was waiting.

'Vasily the Unlucky, did you ask my question?'

'Yes indeed I did. The first man to take the oar from your hands; that is the man who will take your place.'

'God grant it may be soon,' replied the ferryman; and he took Vasily across the river.

So Vasily came back to the house of Marko the Rich. Anastasya welcomed him joyfully, but Marko turned white with rage because the Heathen Dragon had not eaten him.

At last he said, 'Well did you ask my question?'

'Yes indeed I did,' said Vasily. 'Even the Heathen Dragon cannot count all your money; but there is enough to cover the ground for twenty miles around with coins an inch deep.'

'Well, that's true enough. And what strange things did you see on your journey?' For Marko hoped to find out how the boy had escaped from the Heathen Dragon.

'I saw a pillar of gold,' said Vasily the Unlucky, 'which belongs to the son of Marko the Rich; yet it fell at my feet in a heap, saying, "Now I belong to you!" But I am your son-in-law, not your son. What does this mean?'

Now Marko the Rich knew that Vasily was indeed his adopted son, whom he had thrown into the river so many years ago, and when he heard about the gold his eyes lit up with greed.

'I will get that gold for myself,' he thought, 'and get rid of this wretched boy at the same time.'

So he ordered a train of wagons to be harnessed, and bade Vasily the Unlucky set out with him to fetch the gold.

When they came at last to the wide river they started to carry the gold across. They had to make several journeys, for the heap was so big that the ferryman could not carry it all at once.

When the last load had been brought ashore, Marko the Rich rose up.

'Now, Vasily the Unlucky, say your prayers, for your last hour has come!' he cried. 'Many years have I sought your death and you have escaped me. This time I will kill you with my own hands.'

So saying, Marko seized the ferryman's oar and raised it above his head to strike down Vasily where he stood. But as he did so lightning flashed and thunder shook; the oar stuck to his hands and his feet cleaved to the ferryboat, so that he could no longer move. He cursed and struggled with all his strength but nothing helped. So there he had to stay, ferrying back and forth

for no payment until the flesh fell from his hands and the blood ran from bone to bone. That is how he was punished for all his wickedness.

As for Vasily the Unlucky, he returned home with the gold and took possession of all Marko's wealth. He helped the poor and gave food and drink to beggars. Anastasya his wife bore him many children—

And so they lived
For many a year
And never had cause
To shed a tear.

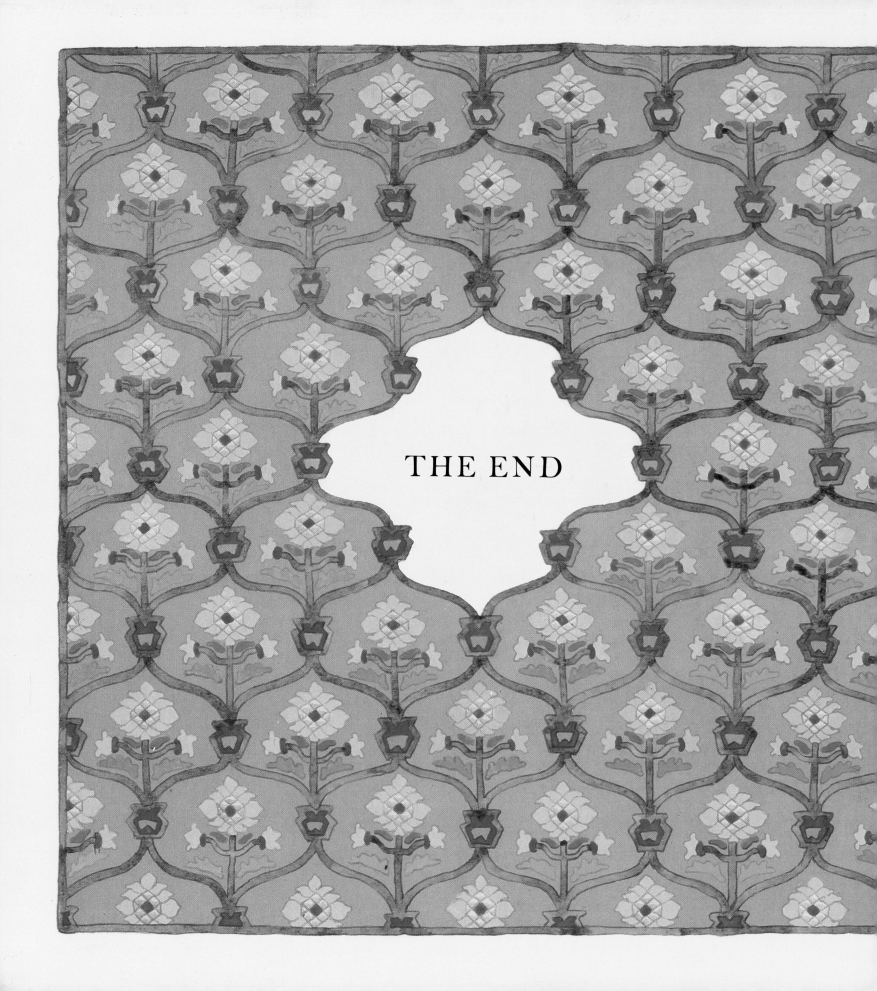

THE END